Spot Bakes a Cake

Eric Hill

It's your dad's on Friday,

birthday
Spot.

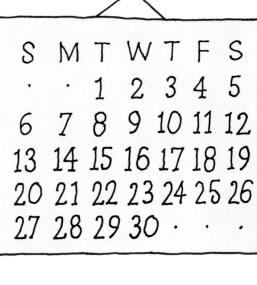

Let's bake a cake!

We have to go

shopping.

Can you

find a bar of chocolate, Spot?

Now we can

make the cake.

Spot! That's enough!

The cake is in the

oven. Help me clean up, Spot!

Can I decorate yet,

the cake
Mum?

Go easy

on the icing, Spot!

This will be a your

nice surprise for dad, Spot.

birthday, Dad!

Did

you make the
cake, Spot?
It's lovely.

Thanks, Dad.
Mum helped
a bit.

PUFFIN BOOKS

Published by the Penguin Group: London, New York,
Australia, Canada, India, New Zealand and South Africa
Penguin Books Ltd, Registered Offices:
80 Strand, London WC2R 0RL, England

www.penguin.com

First published by Frederick Warne & Co., 1994
Published in Puffin Books 1996
19 20 18

Copyright © Eric Hill, 1994
All rights reserved

The moral right of the author has been asserted

Printed and bound in Malaysia

ISBN 0–140–55513–7